Dear Parents and Educators,

Welcome to Penguin Young Readers! As parents and educators, you know that each child develops at his or her own pace—in terms of speech, critical thinking, and, of course, reading. Penguin Young Readers recognizes this fact. As a result, each Penguin Young Readers book is assigned a traditional easy-to-read level (1–4) as well as a Guided Reading Level (A–P). Both of these systems will help you choose the right book for your child. Please refer to the back of each book for specific leveling information. Penguin Young Readers features esteemed authors and illustrators, stories about favorite characters, fascinating nonfiction, and more!

Mo Jackson: Swim, Mo, Swim!

LEVEL **2**

GUIDED READING LEVEL **I**

This book is perfect for a **Progressing Reader** who:
- can figure out unknown words by using picture and context clues;
- can recognize beginning, middle, and ending sounds;
- can make and confirm predictions about what will happen in the text; and
- can distinguish between fiction and nonfiction.

Here are some **activities** you can do during and after reading this book:
- Word Repetition: Reread the story and count how many times you read the following words: *race*, *swim*, *fish*, and *lake*. Then, on a separate sheet of paper, work with the child to write a new sentence for each word.
- Summarize: Work with the child to write a short summary about what happened in the story. What happened in the beginning? What happened in the middle? What happened at the end?

Remember, sharing the love of reading with a child is the best gift you can give!

*This book has been officially leveled by using the F&P Text Level Gradient™ leveling system.

*Penguin Young Readers are leveled by independent reviewers applying the standards developed by Irene Fountas and Gay Su Pinnell in *Matching Books to Readers: Using Leveled Books in Guided Reading*, Heinemann, 1999.

For Barbara and Larry R. Many thanks
for welcoming my grandsons to your pool
for swim lessons. —D.A.A.

For Joseph, Paige, and all the fam. —S.R.

Penguin Young Readers
An imprint of Penguin Random House LLC
New York

First published in the United States of America by Penguin Young Readers,
an imprint of Penguin Random House LLC, 2020

Text copyright © 2020 by David Adler
Illustrations copyright © 2020 by Sam Ricks

Visit us online at penguinrandomhouse.com

LIBRARY OF CONGRESS CATALOGING-IN-PUBLICATION DATA IS AVAILABLE
ISBN 9781984836786

Manufactured in China

1   3   5   7   9   10   8   6   4   2

SWIM, MO, SWIM!

by David A. Adler
illustrated by Sam Ricks

Penguin Young Readers
An Imprint of Penguin Random House LLC

"We're here! We're here!"

Mo Jackson says to

his friend Ken.

"I love Field Day."

Mo and Ken get off the bus.

They join their Field Day group,

the Guppies.

"I hope I win a medal," Ken says.

"I hope the Guppies win

the most medals," Mo says.

"Then we get extra ice cream."

"Stay together," Dan calls out.

Dan is the Guppies' group leader.

The Guppies walk past a large

open field.

BUZZ! BUZZ!

A toy airplane flies just over their heads.

Mo looks up.

He sees lots of kites flying

above the toy airplane.

The Guppies walk by a large lake.

Many people are fishing by the lake.

"Look," Ken says.

"That woman just caught a fish."
There is a basket filled with fish
next to the woman.

"Games and races are first,"

Dan says.

"Then we eat."

He gives Ken a large spoon.

Ken tells Mo,

"I'm in the egg race."

Polly is the Field Day leader.

"*Get set*," she calls out. *"Go!"*

"Go, Ken, go!" Mo shouts.

Ken goes, but he goes too fast.

The egg falls off his spoon.

"Look, I have egg on my shoe,"

he tells Mo.

"And I didn't win a medal."

Mo and Ken cheer for Guppies in the three-legged race,

the potato sack race,

and the backward race.

Mary wins the backward race.

She is the only Guppy

to win a medal.

The Guppies have one medal.

The Hamsters, the Gerbils,

and the Bunnies each also

have one medal.

The last race of the day is

swimming.

That's Mo's race.

"Let's go!" Ken tells Mo.

"We get extra ice cream if you win."

Mo stands on the dock.

"*On your marks,*" Polly says.

"*Get set. Go!*"

The other swimmers
jump in the water.

"Wait for me!" Mo says.

Mo jumps in the water.

He has a late start.

"Swim, Mo!" Ken shouts.

"Swim, Mo, swim!"

the other Guppies shout.

Mo takes nice, even strokes.

His legs are straight

when he kicks.

His form is fine, but he is losing

the race.

Still, Mo takes his nice,

even strokes.

Then Mo feels something

touch his foot.

It tickles.

"Hey!" Mo says.

"Stop that!"

He feels it again.

"Stop that!" Mo shouts.

Mo turns.

A fish is nibbling

on his toe.

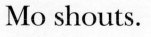

"Get me out of here!"

Mo shouts.

He kicks and kicks.

He moves his arms

faster and faster.

"Go, Mo, go!" Ken shouts.

Mo swings his arms some more. Now his swimming form is not as good, but he is moving quickly through the water.

"Go, Mo, go!" the Guppies shout.

Mo swims past the finish line.

He swims until he reaches

the edge of the lake.

Then he runs out of the water.

"Yay!" the Guppies shout.

Mo stops running.

The lake and the fish

are now far behind him.

"We won!" Dan shouts.

"What did we win?" Mo asks.

"You won the swimming race,"

Dan tells him.

"I did?" Mo asks.

"Yes," Ken tells him.

"You won a medal.

And we won Field Day."

"Kids," Polly calls out.

"Join your groups.

Guppies, gather

around me."

Polly gives Mo his medal.

Polly says, "I didn't know

you could swim so fast."

"I can't," Mo tells her.

"But you did," Polly says.

"You can do lots of things."

At lunch, Mo tells Ken,
"This is my first medal,
and this is my second dish
of ice cream."